The 12 Days
St. Patrick's Day

D0129156

by Jenna Lettice • illustrated by Colleen Madden

A Random House PICTUREBACK® Book

Random House 🏠 New York

Text copyright © 2021 by Jenna Lettice. Cover art and interior illustrations copyright © 2021 by Colleen Madden.
All rights reserved. Published in the United States by Random House Children's Books, a division of
Penguin Random House LLC, 1745 Broadway, New York, NY 10019. Pictureback, Random House,
and the Random House colophon are registered trademarks of Penguin Random House LLC.
rhcbooks.com
Library of Congress Control Number: 2019952898
ISBN 978-0-593-17501-9 (trade) — ISBN 978-0-593-17502-6 (ebook)
MANUFACTURED IN CHINA 10 9 8 7 6 5 4 3 2 1

On the **first** day
of St. Patrick's,
I was lucky to find:

A shamrock
in a field of green.

On the **second** day
of St. Patrick's,
I was lucky to find:

Two pots of gold
and a shamrock
in a field of green.

On the **third** day
of St. Patrick's,
I was lucky to find:

Three top hats,
Two pots of gold,
and a shamrock
in a field of green.

On the **fourth** day
of St. Patrick's,
I was lucky to find:

Four shepherd's pies,
Three top hats,
Two pots of gold,
and a shamrock
in a field of green.

On the **fifth** day
of St. Patrick's,
I was lucky to find:

Five lucky charms!
Four shepherd's pies,
Three top hats,
Two pots of gold,
and a shamrock
in a field of green.

On the **sixth** day
of St. Patrick's,
I was lucky to find:

Six footprints leading,
Five lucky charms!
Four shepherd's pies,
Three top hats,
Two pots of gold,
and a shamrock
in a field of green.

On the **seventh** day
of St. Patrick's,
I was lucky to find:

Seven colors shining,
Six footprints leading,

Five lucky charms!
Four shepherd's pies,
Three top hats,
Two pots of gold,
and a shamrock
in a field of green.

On the **eighth** day
of St. Patrick's,
I was lucky to find:

Eight milkshakes melting,
Seven colors shining,
Six footprints leading,

Five lucky charms!
Four shepherd's pies,
Three top hats,
Two pots of gold,
and a shamrock
in a field of green.

On the **ninth** day
of St. Patrick's,
I was lucky to find:

Nine pipers playing,
Eight milkshakes melting,
Seven colors shining,

Six footprints leading,
Five lucky charms!
Four shepherd's pies,
Three top hats,
Two pots of gold,
and a shamrock
in a field of green.

On the **tenth** day
of St. Patrick's,
I was lucky to find:

Ten makers crafting,
Nine pipers playing,
Eight milkshakes melting,
Seven colors shining,
Six footprints leading,
Five lucky charms!
Four shepherd's pies,
Three top hats,
Two pots of gold,
and a shamrock
in a field of green.

On the **eleventh** day
of St. Patrick's,
I was lucky to find:

Eleven dancers stepping,

Ten makers crafting,
Nine pipers playing,
Eight milkshakes melting,
Seven colors shining,
Six footprints leading,

Five lucky charms!
Four shepherd's pies,
Three top hats,
Two pots of gold,
and a shamrock
in a field of green.

On the **twelfth** day
of St. Patrick's,
I was lucky to find:

Twelve leprechauns marching,
Eleven dancers stepping,
Ten makers crafting,
Nine pipers playing,
Eight milkshakes melting,
Seven colors shining,
Six footprints leading,
Five lucky charms!
Four shepherd's pies,
Three top hats,
Two pots of gold . . .

me I'm
🍀 ♥ !

. . . and a shamrock in a field of green.

Happy St. Patrick's Day!